MOOSE IN THE GARDEN

Moose in the Garden
Text copyright © 1990 by Nancy White Carlstrom
Illustrations copyright © 1990 by Lisa Desimini
Printed in the U.S.A. All rights reserved.
Typography by Andrew J. Rhodes
1 2 3 4 5 6 7 8 9 10
First Edition

Library of Congress Cataloging-in-Publication Data
Carlstrom, Nancy White.
  Moose in the garden / by Nancy White Carlstrom ; illustrated by
Lisa Desimini.
    p. cm.
  Summary: A young child is delighted when Papa Moose visits the
garden and eats almost all the vegetables.
  ISBN 0-06-021015-X : $. — ISBN 0-06-021014-1 (lib. bdg.) : $
  [1. Gardens—Fiction. 2. Vegetables—Fiction. 3. Moose—
Fiction.] I. Desimini, Lisa, ill. II. Title.
PZ7.C21684Mo   1990   89-29407
[E]—dc20   CIP
                                                             AC

For the Tape Family,
Jeanne, Walt, Ken, and Carl,
who share our garden and its moose
n.w.c.

For my grandmothers,
Rose and Katherine
l.d.

NANCY WHITE CARLSTROM

MOOSE IN THE GARDEN

PAINTINGS BY LISA DESIMINI

HARPER & ROW, PUBLISHERS

This is our garden.

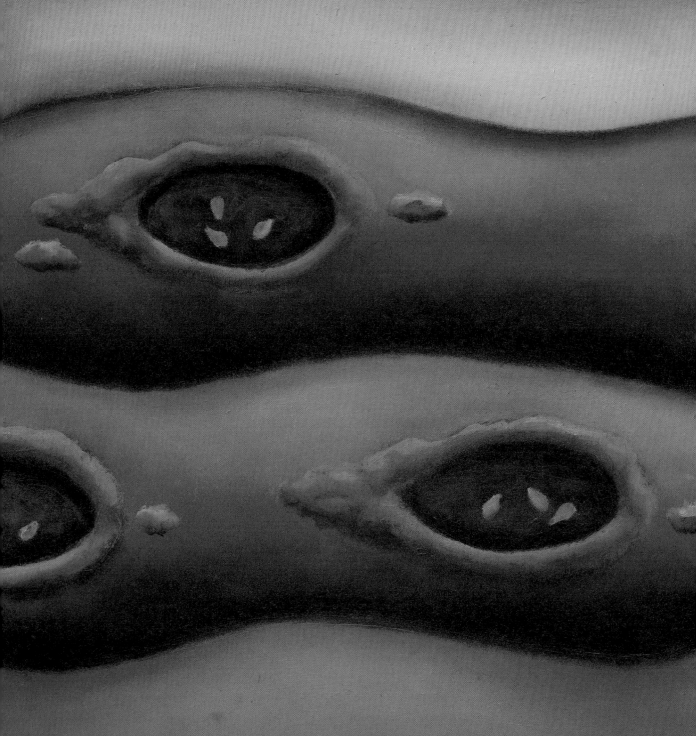

These are the seeds
we put in the dirt of our garden.

**These are the seeds
we put in the dirt of our garden,
warmed by the sun.**

7

These are the seeds
we put in the dirt of our garden,

warmed by the sun,
watered by rain.

These are the plants.

These are the plants
that grow in our garden.

10

The plants grow and grow and grow.

This is a moose.

This is a moose
who walks through the woods.

This is a moose
who walks through the woods
and comes to our garden.

This is a moose
who walks through the woods
and comes to our garden,
looking for something to eat.

This is a hungry moose
eating up our garden.

The moose eats and eats and eats.

"Oh, no!" says my mother
who looks out the window.

"Oh, go!" says my father
who looks out the door.

The moose is eating the broccoli!

"Oh, go!" says my mother
who runs from the window.

"Oh, no!" says my father
who runs out the door.

The moose is eating the cabbages and cauliflower!

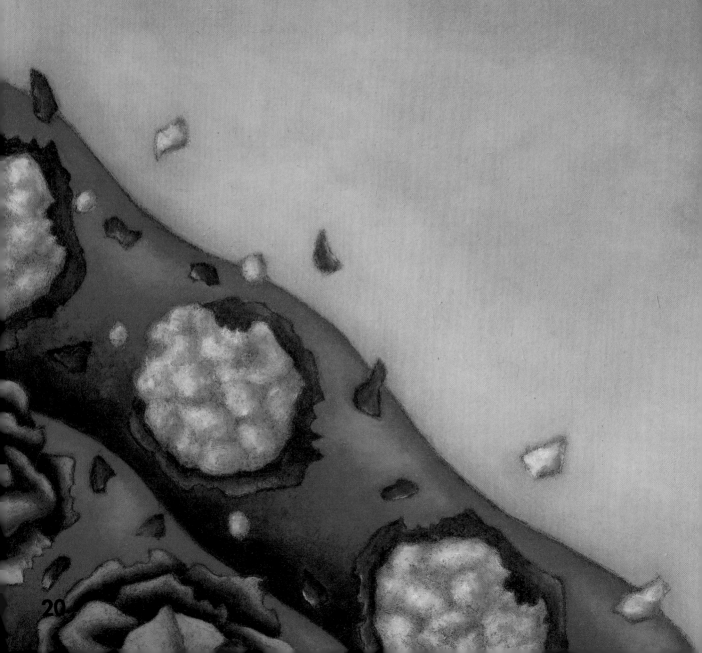

These are the plants
that are left in our garden.

These are the plants
that are left in our garden
that the moose does not want.

These are the vegetables
that grow on the plants
that are left in our garden
that the moose does not want.

Where are the cabbages?

Where are the broccoli and cauliflower?

Gone, gone, gone!

Gone with the moose.

Only the pictures are left.

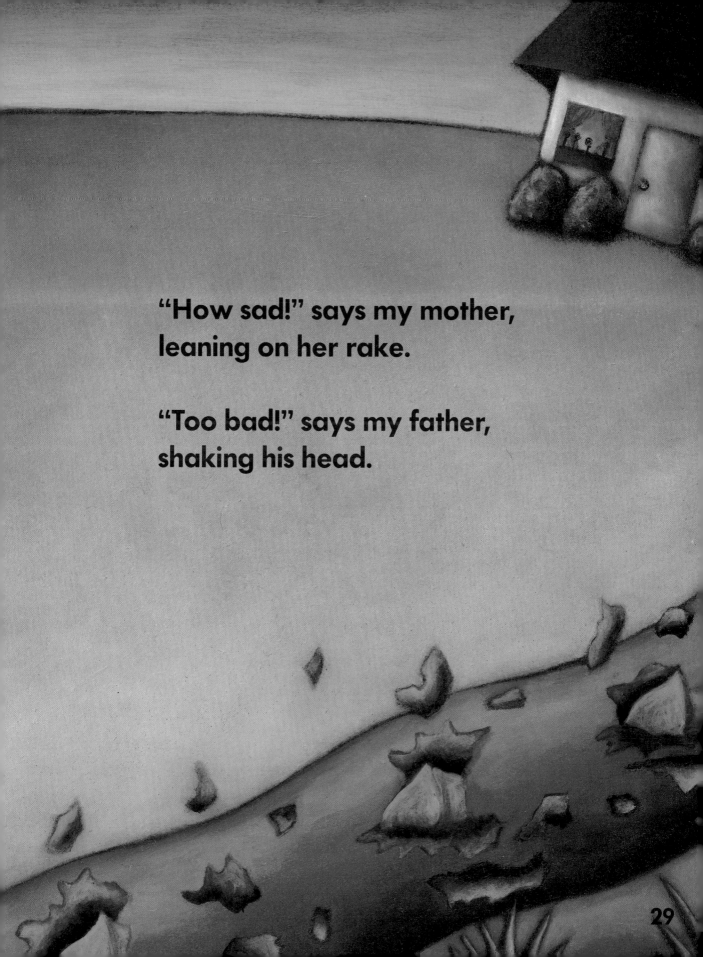

"How sad!" says my mother,
leaning on her rake.

"Too bad!" says my father,
shaking his head.

"I'm glad!" I say,
singing to myself.

GARDEN SONG

I like carrots and peas,
lettuce and beans,
tomatoes, potatoes
and cucumbers, too.

But not cauliflower
or big cabbage heads
or broccoli! Not for me
Papa Moose, thank you.

Next time you visit,
zucchini—don't miss it!
Eat up, take twenty!
There's PLENTY!